Hey
Jack!
KT-415-980

The Worst Sleepover
first published in 2012
this edition published in 2017 by
Hardie Grant Egmont
Ground Floor, Building 1, 658 Church Street
Richmond, Victoria 3121, Australia
www.hardiegrantegmont.com.au

A CiP record for this title is available from the National Library of Australia.

Design by Stephanie Spartels
Typesetting by Michaela Stone

Printed in China through Asia Pacific Offset

1 3 5 4 2

By Sally Rippin

Illustrated by Stephanie Spartels

hardie grant EGMONT

Wiggly Mood

This is Jack. Today Jack is in a wiggly mood. He is wiggling and jiggling so much he can't keep still.

Tonight Jack is going to
his friend Jem's house.
Jack has never had
a sleepover at Jem's
before.
Jem has a Wii and a
PlayStation *and* a
computer in his room.
Jack and Jem are going
to play games *all night*.
Jack can't wait.

At last, it is time to go. Jack's dad drives to Jem's house. Jem opens the front door.

'Hey, Jack,' Jem grins. 'You're *finally* here!'

'Jem is *very* excited,' says Jem's mum to Jack.

'Me too!' says Jack.

The two boys run into

Jem's room.

'See you tomorrow!'

Jack's dad calls.

Jem's room is very cool. First Jack and Jem race cars on the PlayStation. Next they play sport on the Wii. Then they go on the computer to build cities. It is lots of fun.

'Let's go outside and play soccer,' says Jem after a while.

'Nah,' says Jack.

'How about we build a cubby, then?' says Jem.

Jack shakes his head. He is too busy playing on the computer.

'Well, *I'm* going outside!' Jem says crossly. He **STOMPS** out of the room.

Hmm, thinks Jack.

What's wrong with Jem?

He quickly finishes

his game. Then he goes

outside to look for Jem.

Jem is in the garden.

He is kicking a soccer

ball against the fence.

Jack goes over to see

if Jem is OK.

But just then, Jem's mum calls them for dinner.

Jem rushes past Jack without even looking at him. Jack follows him inside. He feels confused. Jem is acting very strangely!

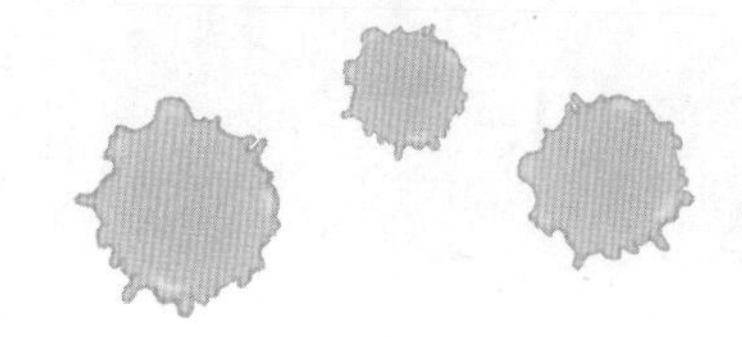

Jack and Jem sit up

at the table.

'I hope you like

spicy food, Jack?'

Jem's mum asks.

'Um, sure,' says Jack. He is too shy to tell her he has never tried spicy food before.

Jem's mum puts a big dish on the table.

'Not curry again!'
Jem grumbles.

'Jem,' says his mum
crossly. 'You'll eat
what you are given.'

Jem's mum puts some
rice on Jack's plate.
Phew! Jack thinks.
I like rice.

But then she spoons
curry over the rice.

Jack can see chicken,
carrots and potatoes
in the yellow sauce.
Jack doesn't like
carrots much. He feels
nervous.

Jack looks at Jem. He is
eating everything. Jack
pokes his fork into a
piece of chicken. He puts
it into his mouth.

Suddenly his mouth starts to burn.

His eyes water.

'Oh dear,' says Jem's mum. 'Is the curry too hot for you, Jack?'

Jack swallows the chicken. Then he takes a big drink of water to try to cool his mouth.

'Maybe a little bit,' he says to Jem's mum in a squeaky voice.

Jem giggles.

Jack frowns. *Why is Jem laughing at me?* he thinks. His cheeks get red and **hot**.

'That's all right, Jack,' she says. 'You don't have to eat it. I don't know what I'm going to give you for dinner, though.'

‘I like rice,’ Jack says shyly.

‘Can I just have rice, too?’ Jem asks.

Jem's mum shakes her head. 'Jack is our guest,' she says. 'He is allowed to eat what he wants. You need to finish your dinner as usual.' She gives Jack a bowl of plain rice.

'Aw, that's not fair!' says Jem crossly.

'Sorry,' whispers Jack to Jem. But Jem pretends not to hear.

Jem eats all his dinner without looking at Jack once.

Jack can't understand why Jem is acting so strangely.

'Would you boys like to watch a DVD before you go to bed?' asks Jem's mum. 'I have to do some work.'

'Yes, please!' says Jack.

'Whatever. I don't care,' says Jem **grumpily**. He sits down on the couch next to Jack.

The two boys watch a movie. The movie is very funny, but Jem doesn't laugh once.

Jack wishes he was back at home. At least when he watches a movie with his mum and dad, they laugh at the funny bits.

Jack feels a little bit grumpy with Jem.

Jack had been looking forward to this sleepover for a long time. It was supposed to be the **best** sleepover ever. Instead it has turned out to be the worst!

After the movie
it is time for bed.
Jack and Jem change
into their pyjamas
and brush their teeth.

Jem's mum comes
to say goodnight.

'Hope you boys are
having fun,' she says.
'Don't stay up too late
talking, will you?'

Jack lies in the dark.
He wishes his mum and
dad were here to kiss
him goodnight.

Instead there is just grumpy old Jem who won't even talk to him.

Jack feels lonely.
He wonders if it is
too late to call his
mum and dad to
come and get him.

Just then, he hears
a noise. A sniffly, snuffly
sound. Jack realises
Jem is crying!

'What's the matter?'
asks Jack.

Jem stops crying.

'Nothing,' he says.

Now Jack feels **cross**.

'Why won't you

talk to me?' he says.

Jem sits up in bed.

He turns on his

bedside lamp.

'You are the boringest

friend ever!' he shouts.

'What?' yells Jack.

'No, I'm not. *You* are!

You said we could

play games all night

and now you don't

want to!'

Jack is so angry he feels

like he might explode.

Suddenly Jem bursts out

laughing.

'What?' says Jack.

'You look funny,'

Jem giggles.

'I've never seen you
look that cross before.
You look like an
angry monkey.'

Jack tries not to smile,
but Jem's laughter
makes his mouth
twitch.

'Well, *you* look like a
grumpy gorilla!' he says.

Jem laughs. 'You should have seen your face when you tasted Mum's curry,' he says. 'You went all red like a baboon's bottom.'

Jack frowns. 'I haven't eaten spicy food before,' he says. 'It's not my fault!'

'Don't worry,' Jem says kindly. 'You have to get used to it. I've been eating curries since I was a baby!'

'Do you really think I'm a boring friend?' Jack asks.

‘Of course not!’ says Jem. ‘I just wanted you to come and play soccer, that’s all.’

‘But you have so many cool video games,’ says Jack. ‘Don’t you want to play with them?’

Jem shakes his head. ‘Not all the time.

Usually it's just me
and Mum at home.
I have to play video
games by myself.
It gets boring.
And she never
wants to play soccer.
That's why I was so
excited about you
coming over. Finally,
someone to play with!'

Jack feels bad.

He might not have

any video games, but

he always has someone

to play with – his dog

Scraps, his best friend

Billie, even his mum

and dad sometimes.

He was so **excited**

to play Jem's games

that he hadn't thought about what Jem might want to do.

'All right,' says Jack. 'Tomorrow it's your turn to decide what we play.'

'Cool!' says Jem. 'But don't you want to beat my high score on the computer first?'

‘Nah,’ says Jack, smiling.
‘I think I’d like to
beat you at soccer.
That sounds like
much more fun!’